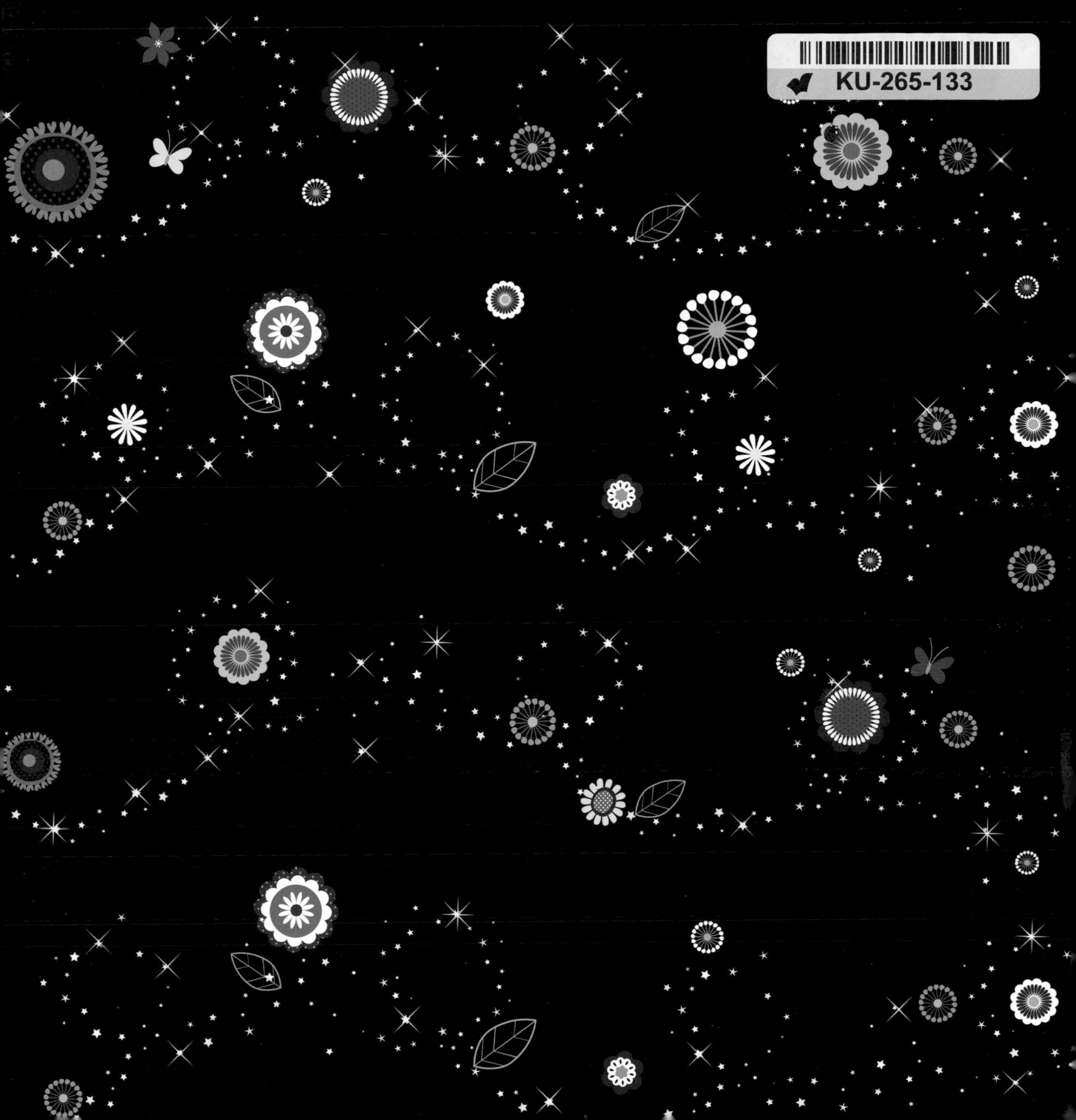

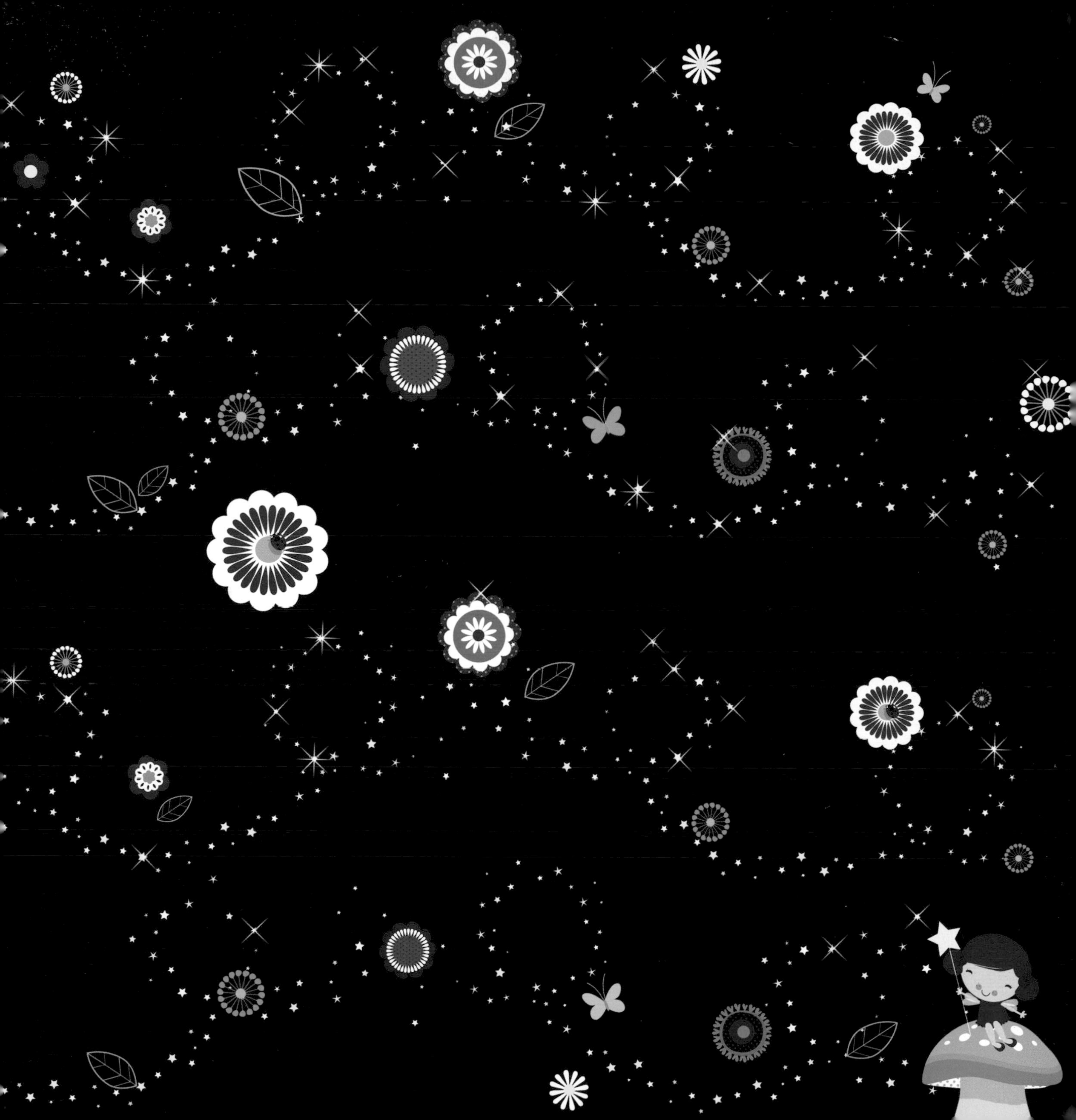

For: Maisey

First published in 2015 by Rockpool Children's Books Ltd.
This edition published in 2015 by Rockpool Children's Books Ltd.
in association with Albury Books.

Albury Court, Albury, Thame, OX9 2LP

For orders: Kuperard Publishers & Distributors
office@kuperard.co.uk | 020 8446 2440

A CIP catalogue record of this book is available
from the British Library.

Printed and bound in Turkey

ISBN 978-1-906081-97-3 (Paperback)

Sam Walshaw

Little Fairies

Poppy's Magic

It was early morning in the garden,
and the fairies were just waking up.

Poppy woke first. It was her turn
to collect the sweet, gooey honey
from the bumblebees
at the bottom of the garden.
The fairies loved honey
for breakfast.

As Poppy got to the
bottom of the garden,
she was puzzled.
There was no busy buzzing
around the hive.
Everything was
strangely quiet.

"Those lazy bees must
have slept in," thought Poppy.
"I'd better wake them up!"

Poppy knocked on the hive door.
Knock, knock, KNOCK!
There was no answer.
She crept inside.

"Oh dear," she said. "Whatever's wrong?"

"Aachooo!" sneezed a nearby bee.
"We all have a cold and a runny nose
– and we can't collect any pollen to
make your breakfast honey!"

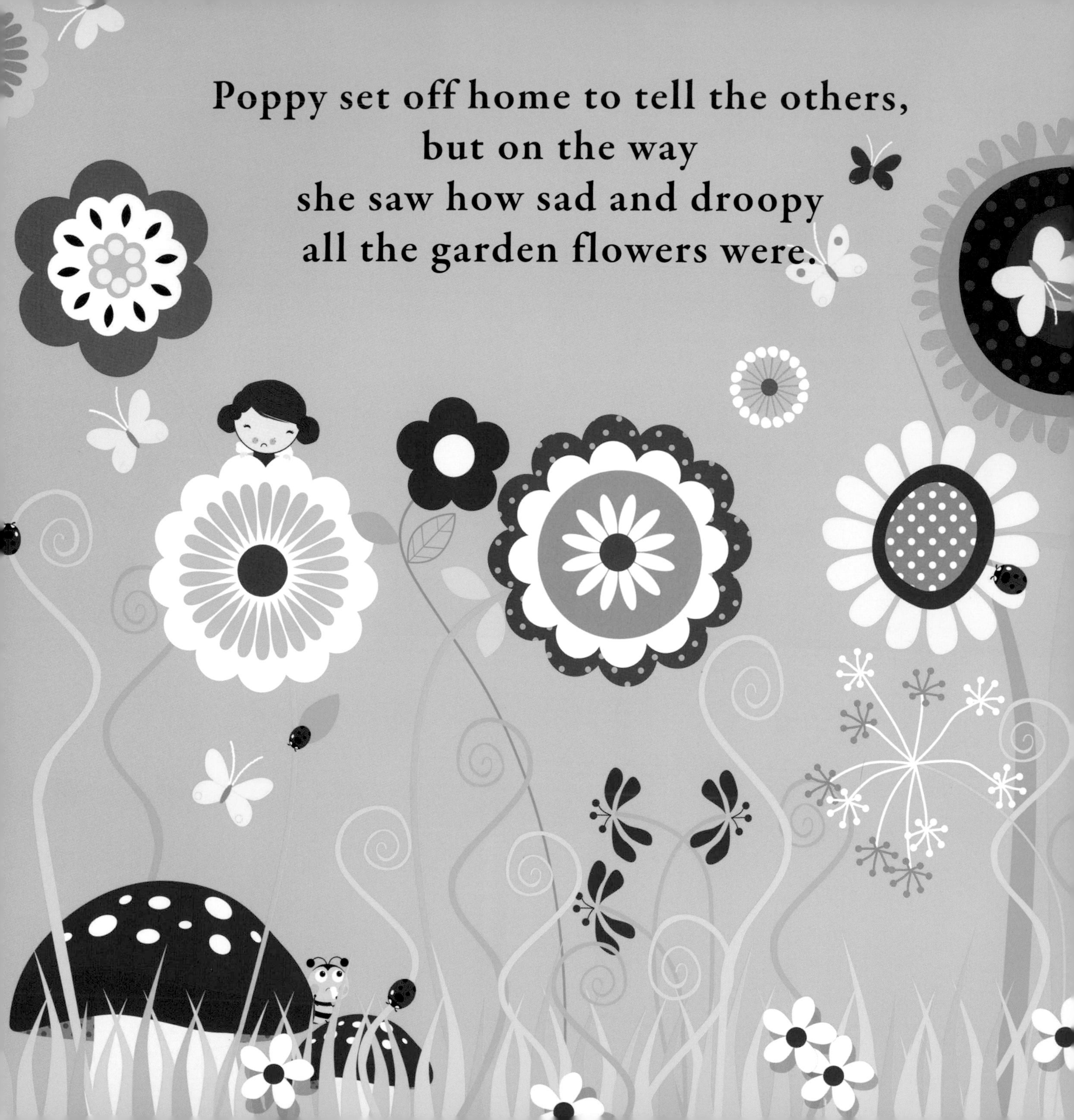

Poppy set off home to tell the others,
but on the way
she saw how sad and droopy
all the garden flowers were.

"The flowers have too much pollen – it's making them wilt," thought Poppy, glumly.

Poppy flew back as fast as her wings could carry her, to tell Rose and Ivy what had happened.

“Oh no, what are we going to do?” wailed Rose and Ivy. “Don’t worry! I’ll collect up all the pollen,” said Poppy. “Meanwhile, I need you two to take care of those poor, poorly bumblebees.”

With a wave of her wand, Poppy trilled,
"Time for some fairy magic!"

Poppy flew round and round
the garden,
sprinkling magic dust
on every flower and tree.

She sprinkled all day long,
touching every single petal and leaf.

The sun was setting when Poppy finished.
She flew wearily back to the hive.

"We thought you were bringing all the pollen, Poppy," moaned Rose and Ivy.

"The bees need it to make their honey, and the flowers have too much to carry. They look even worse than before!"

"Don't worry. Just wait and see," smiled Poppy.

As the sun sank and the moon rose, Poppy whispered her magic spell.

“Pollen, pollen –
shine like gold. Let’s
help the bees –
they have a cold!”

Then something magical happened!
The flowers began to stand up straight.
They shook and jiggled about
as if they were dancing.

As they shook, the pollen rose out of them and floated around in the clear night sky, like millions of tiny golden stars.

Poppy flew through the air,
followed by the magic,
sparkling flower dust.

"This way,"
she whispered,
guiding the
pollen to
the hive.

Like golden snow, the pollen settled into the bumblebees' waiting buckets.

By now, the bees felt much better, and the hive was busily buzzing with excitement again.

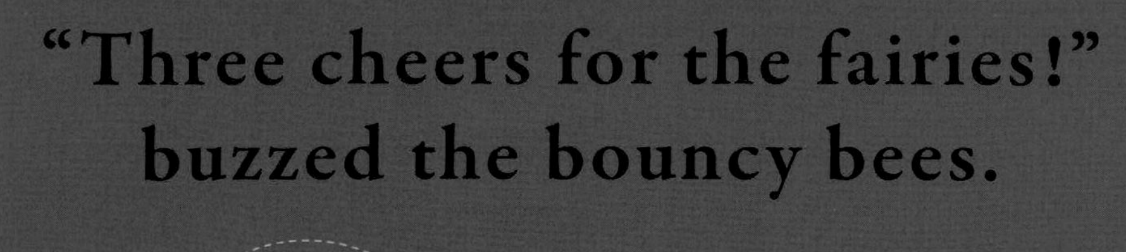

"Three cheers for the fairies!"
buzzed the bouncy bees.

The bees were so pleased, they gave the lucky fairies an extra big jar of honey to take home. After all, it was almost breakfast time again!

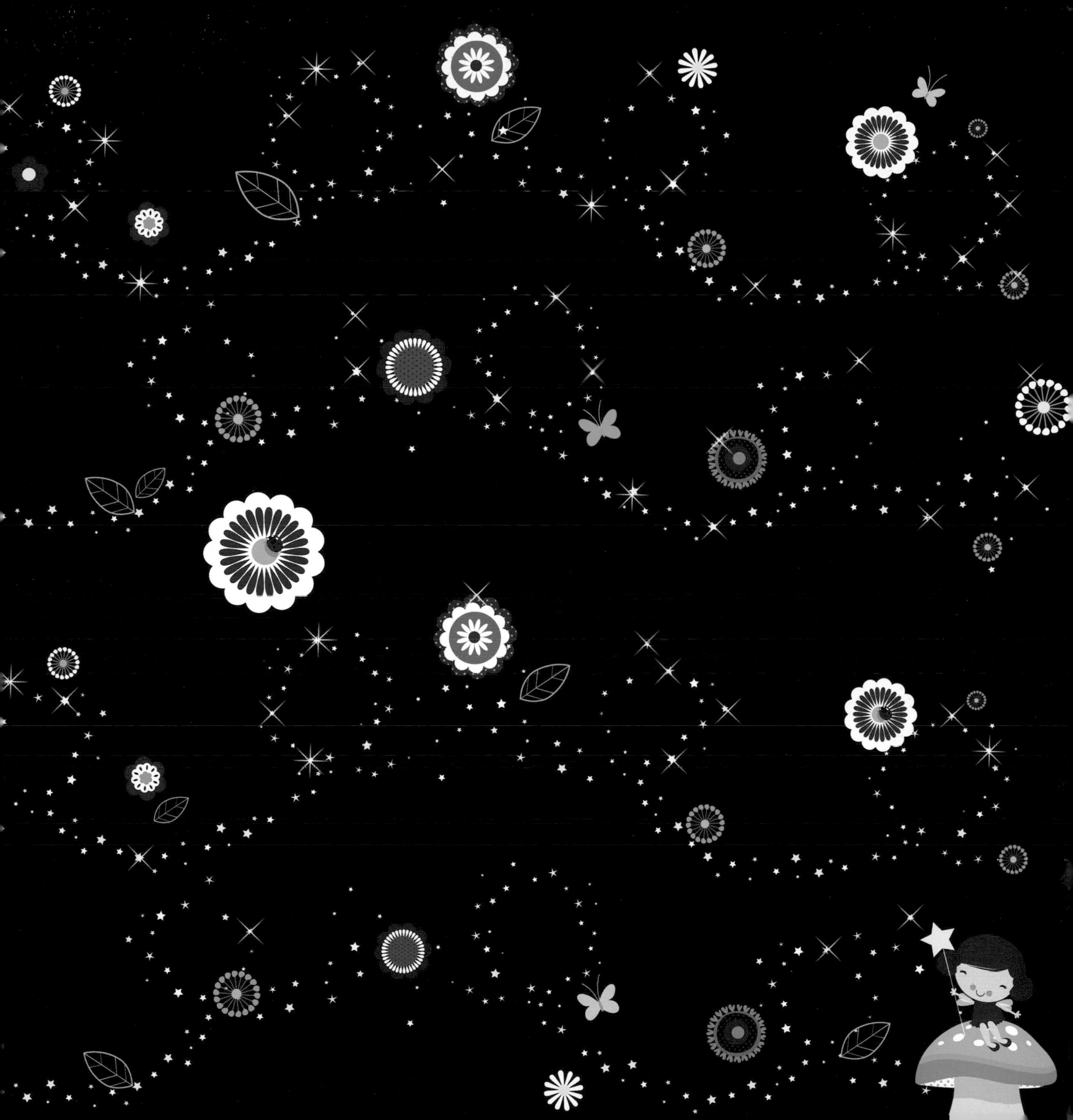